The Brigade

The Brigade

A Collection Of Short Stories

A.D. Covington

This is a work of fiction. Names, characters, places and incidents either are the product of the author's imagination or are used fictitiously, and any resemblance to any actual persons, living or dead, events, or locales is entirely coincidental.

This book was printed in the United States of America.

To order additional copies of this book, contact:
Xlibris Corporation
1-888-795-4274
www.Xlibris.com
Orders@Xlibris.com
47709

Contents

THE BRIGADE

A Collection of Short Stories

This is a collection of five short stories. The first story is Alana's Swing. Alana and Pinky teach Scooter a lesson he won't forget. In Billy and the Witch, Billy sets out to find a friend to play with. Along the way, he encounters a witch. In the third story, the Missing pie, Jody finds out that it doesn't pay to steal. In The Adventure of Farmer Jack, the farmer learns that one dog just isn't enough. And in the last story, The Field House Meets the House Mouse, two mice, Bill and Will, are determined to keep their sister away from the field mouse because she is the only one who can handle the big cat.

Alana's New Swing

One day after school, Alana found a surprise waiting for her at home. Her Father had built a swing for her. Two of her friends, Pinky and Scooter who was also at her house were just as excited as Alana was. Pinky waited patiently for Alana to take her turn riding on the swing but Scooter's patience ran thin. He became angry and violent. The girls decided to teach Scooter a lesson. Together they came up with a plan that would make him think twice before reacting that way again. He has to learn that in order to have friends he must first have patience.

One evening when Alana got home from school her father had built her a swing. "Daddy, that's the best looking swing I have ever seen. Is it for me?" Alana asked.

"Yes it is" said her father.

Alana, Pinkie, and Scooter went outside to play on the swing. "I'm first said Scooter."

"No I'm first". Said Pinkie,

But Alana replied, "Well since it's my swing I'm riding first."

"I'm sorry Alana you're right. You should ride first," said Pinkie as she got out of the swing. Then Pinkie began to push Alana in the swing. Now it was Pinkie's time to swing. But Scooter was very impatience.

"When will it be my turn?" asked Scooter

"As soon as Pinkie finish swinging then you can swing," said Alana.

But Scooter didn't want to wait any longer. He demanded to swing right then, so he pushed Pinkie out of the swing, kicked Alana on the leg, and then ran home.

"I'm not playing with Scooter anymore," said Pinkie as she got up off the ground.

"He should be taught a lesson. Let's go tell his mother," Said Alana.

Then the two girls ran down the streets behind Scooter.

"Mrs. Harper, Mrs. Harper" shouted the two girls, "Scooter pushed me out of the swing" shouted Pinkie.

"He kicked me on the leg," Added Alana.

Mrs. Harper began calling Scooter but there was no answer. Scooter had found a nice place to hide. Mrs. Harper called for him again, stills no answer.

"Alana and Pinkie will you help me find him Asked Mrs. Harper?"

They looked all through the house. Mrs. Harper looked in the bedrooms, Pinkie looked in the living room and Alana looked in the kitchen. Suddenly Alana heard a noise coming from under the kitchen sink. She opened the cabinet door and there was Scooter sitting there with a big smile on his face.

"Mrs. Harper, come in here!" Shouted Alana!

Mrs. Harper and Pinkie ran into the kitchen.

"There he is under the kitchen sink," said Alana.

"Come from under there right now Scooter" said Mrs. Harper, "How many times have I told you about fighting?"

Then she took him into the other room and gave him a spanking. Alana and Pinkie went back down the street to Alana's house so they could finish Swinging After a few minutes had passed they looked around and Scooter was running back to her house also.

He came to apologize to the girls. "I'm sorry for pushing you out of the swing Pinkie, and I'm sorry for kicking you Alana. Do you accept my apology?"

"We do" both girls said.

"You will still have to wait your turn for the swing," said Alana.

So the children played together the rest of the day.

The End

Billy and the Witch

When Billy arrived home from school, he wanted something to do. So he decided to play a game of catch but he didn't have anyone to play with him.

"Dad, will you play ball with me?" asked Billy.

"I don't have time to play," replied his dad. "Ask your mother."

"Mom, will you play ball with me?" asked Billy.

"I have to finish cooking," replied his mother. So Billy went outside. He saw John.

"John, would you play ball with me?" asked Billy.

"I don't have time," replied John. He saw Mary.

"Mary, will you play ball with me?" asked Billy.

"I have to get ready for my date," replied Mary. So Billy began bouncing his ball up and down.

"I've got an idea," thought Billy to himself. "I'll go off into the woods and play with the animals."

So off into the woods Billy went, bouncing his ball up and down. Billy saw a butterfly resting on a flower.

"Mr. Butterfly, would you play catch with me?" asked Billy.

"No," said the butterfly. "I'm much too little to play catch. That big ball will crush me and break my wings."

So off Billy went further into the woods. Billy met a turtle.

"Mr. Turtle, would you play catch with me?" asked Billy.

"No," said the turtle. "I'm too slow to play catch and the ball may break my shell." So off Billy went bouncing his ball up and down, hoping to find someone to play with. He met a rabbit.

"Mr. Rabbit, would you play catch with me?"

"No," said the rabbit. "I have to finish gathering my carrots." So off Billy went bouncing his ball up and down, up and down. He met a squirrel.

"Miss Squirrel, would you play catch with me?"

"No," said the squirrel. "I have to finish gathering my nuts for supper."

So off Billy went further into the woods hoping to find someone to play with. He saw a house in the woods. Billy knocked on the door. The witch looked through the window.

"A little boy." she said in a low voice. "Just what I need a little boy though the witch to her self."

The witch went to the door. "Who is it?" she asked in a low voice.

"My name is Billy." replied the boy. "Would you play catch with me?"

The witch opens the door. "Come in," she said. "Sure, I'll play catch with you."

So the witch took the ball in her hand.

"I'll throw the ball into the pot of water and you jump in and get it."

"I have never played catch like that before," said Billy.

"This is a new game of catch," said the witch. "When you jump into the water, throw the ball back to me." The witch threw the ball into the pot of water. Billy then jumped into the big pot of water.

"Throw it back to me." said the witch with a sneaky smile.

Billy threw the ball back to the witch, before Billy could get out of the big pot; the witch put a big top over the pot. She then built a fire under the pot.

"What are you doing?" asked Billy in a frightened voice.

"You are going to be the meat for my stew," said the witch.

"You tricked me," said the little boy. "Help!" the boy cried.

"There's no one here to help you," said the witch.

"You tricked me," said Billy." But the witch did not know that the butterfly was flying around the flower.

Help" he yelled again.

The butterfly heard Billy calling for help. So the butterfly flew away to find some help. He saw the squirrel.

"Miss Squirrel, Billy is being cooked by the mean witch," said the butterfly.

The squirrel hurried to the witch's house. The butterfly saw the rabbit.

"Billy is being cooked by the mean witch," said the butterfly. So the rabbit hurried to the witch's house. The butterfly saw the turtle.

"Help!" said the butterfly. "Billy is being cook by the witch."

So they hurried to the witch's house to save Billy. The rabbit knocked on the door. The witch looked out of her window.

"A rabbit, squirrel, turtle, and a butterfly." said the witch to herself.

"Come in" said the witch. "What do you all want?"

"We want to play catch with you," said the rabbit.

"I'll use them in my stew." said the witch.

The witch opened another pot of water.

"When I throw the ball into the water, jump in and get it," said the witch.

The witch threw the ball into the pot of water. The rabbit jumped into the pot of water. The witch went to put the top on the water. The squirrel then pushed the witch into the pot of water. The rabbit jumped out. The rabbit, squirrel and turtle put the top on the pot of water with the witch inside. The butterfly watched patiently as the rabbit let the boy out of the pot of water.

"Thank you, Mr. Rabbit." said Billy in a very happy voice. "Thank you all." explained the boy. So they escaped the house as fast as they could.

"I'll play catch with you, Billy." said Mr. Rabbit.

"And so will I." said Miss. Squirrel, Mr. Turtle and Mr. Butterfly.

So the butterfly, the turtle, the rabbit and the squirrel played catch with Billy.

"It's getting late," said Billy. "I have to go home now."

"Bye." said the butterfly, the turtle, the rabbit and the squirrel.

So off Billy went bouncing his ball up and down. When Billy arrived at home, his dad, mother, brother, and sister played catch with him until it was to dark to see.

The End

The Missing Pie

It was a pretty autumn morning. The leaves were falling off the trees, and the birds were humming a beautiful song. Mother Rabbit was in the kitchen making breakfast. "Breakfast is ready!" she called to Papa Rabbit. "Jody, Sis, come and get breakfast!" called Mother Rabbit.

Everyone sat down to the table and had breakfast. Afterwards, the kids went on with their daily routines. Jody went outside to play; Sis helped Mother Rabbit put away the dishes, while Papa Rabbit sat in his rocking chair watching T.V.

"Mother, can I have a pie for my birthday instead of a cake?" asked Sis.

"Sure you can." said Mother Rabbit. "We will go to the market and buy some apples to make some apple pies," she said. So Mother Rabbit and Sis finished the dishes and started on their way to town to buy some apples.

Jody was outside bouncing his ball up and down. "Papa, can I go to Randy's house?" Randy was Jody's friend who lived about a half mile down the road.

"Yes," said Papa Rabbit. "But be careful and don't go into Mr. Black's garden."

Mr. Black had the biggest garden in the county and he didn't like rabbits coming in his garden eating his carrots and greens. So Jody Rabbit started to Randy Rabbit's house. Along the way, he passed by Mr. Black's garden. He imagined how good the carrots and greens would taste if he ate some. Jody looked around but he didn't see Mr. Black in the garden. He even looked toward the house; there was still no sign of the farmer, so Jody picked a carrot and began eating it. He ate one and then another one.

"Get out of my garden!" shouted Farmer Black.

Jody looked up and saw the man coming after him. Jody jumped up with the carrot he was eating and ran as fast as he could to Randy's house. Jody's parents had told him many times not to steal but he had disobeyed them.

Mother Rabbit and Sis were in the kitchen baking apple pies for the party. Papa Rabbit was still watching T.V. When Mother Rabbit finished baking a pie, she would put it in the window to cool.

"Those sure are some pretty pies," said Karen the bird. She was up in a tree in front of the kitchen window. "Why are you baking so many pies?" asked the bird.

"They are for the birthday party," replied Mother Rabbit.

"Whose birthday is it?" Karen asked.

"It's mine, and you're invited," said Sis.

Later that day, Jody and Randy were on their way to Jody's house. When they passed by Farmer Black's garden Randy wanted to get some carrots.

"Let's get some carrots," suggested Randy.

"Not me," said Jody. "Mr. Black already chased me out once." Jody turned and walked away; that made Randy change his mind.

When the two boys arrived at Jody's house, they saw the apple pies in the window. "Those sure are some good looking pies," said Randy.

"They are for my sister's birthday party," said Jody.

"But there are three in the window and she's still baking more." Randy explained. "Let's get one of them; she won't miss it," he said.

After thinking about Randy's idea, Jody said, "Okay." "But if we get in trouble, I'm blaming you." So Jody Rabbit eased up to the window, snatched one of the pies, and ran around the corner of the house.

He did not know that Karen the bird was watching him until she started singing, "missing pie, missing pie."

When Mother Rabbit heard Karen she looked out the window and saw Jody running with the pie. "Bring that pie back here!" She shouted.

Sis whispered and told Papa Rabbit what had happened.

Papa got up and went outside to look for Jody. When he found Jody, he and Randy were in a corner eating the pie. "How many times have I told you about taking things that don't belong to you, Asked papa rabbit?"

Jody didn't say a word.

"You go home Randy, and Jody, you come with me!" Papa Rabbit commanded.

So the two Rabbits went into the house. Mother Rabbit was very angry at Jody's behavior. "You go to your room and don't come out, not even for the party," she said.

So that night Papa Rabbit, Mother Rabbit, Karen the bird, and some of their friends gave Sis the best party she ever had. But Jody Rabbit had to spend the whole evening in his room.

The End

The Adventure of Farmer Jack

There was a farmer who had the largest farm in the county. He had chickens, cows, horses, goats, ducks; almost any animal that you raise on a farm.

One morning Farmer Jack went out to feed the chickens. He heard a noise out in the chicken house. Then Farmer Jack went back into the house to get his gun. He then shot two times into the air. The fox ran out of the chicken house, up the hill, and into the woods.

That night Farmer Jack was getting ready for bed when he heard a noise coming from the chicken house. "It's that fox again," said the farmer. "What am I going to do about that fox?" So, the farmer jumped out of bed, put on his pants and boots, and hurried out of the house. He ran out to the chicken house yelling, "Get out of there fox! Get out of there fox!" When the farmer reached the chicken house the fox was gone. Up the hill and into the woods, the fox ran.

The next day the farmer went to town. He saw a pet shop across the street. Farmer Jack went into the pet shop. "I would like to buy a dog," said the farmer.

"What kind of dog would you like?" asked the shop owner.

Farmer Jack replied, "Just a regular watch dog. A good dog for chasing away foxes."

When evening came, the fox was in the chicken house again. The dog started barking then he chased the fox up the hill and into the woods. But the dog did not come back. "Where is that dog?" said Farmer Jack. "It's been hours since he chased that fox away. I guess I'll go into town and get another one," said the farmer.

The next day the farmer went back to the pet shop. "I want to buy another dog," said the farmer.

"What happened to the other one?" asked the shop owner.

"He chased the fox into the woods and never returned."

So the farmer bought another dog. That evening the fox was out in the chicken house again. The new dog started barking, and he chased the fox up the hill and into the woods. But the dog never returned. "Where is that dog?" said the farmer. "I guess I'll go into town and buy another one tomorrow."

The next day the farmer went back to the pet shop. "I want to buy another dog said the farmer."

"Did you lose the second dog too?" asked the shop owner.

"Yes," said the farmer. So Farmer Jack bought a third dog and took him home.

That evening the fox was back again. The dog began to bark, and he chased the fox up the hill and into the woods. Once again, the dog never returned.

The farmer went back to the pet shop to buy a fourth dog. "I want to buy another dog," said the farmer.

"Did you lose the third dog too?" asked the shop owner.

"Yes, I did," said the farmer.

"Your dogs came back to the pet shop. That's why you could not find them," said the shop owner.

So the farmer took all three dogs home with him. That evening the fox was in the chicken house again. The dogs started barking, and they chased the fox up the hill and into the woods. The dogs chased the fox all the way to the pet shop. The shop owner now had three dogs and a fox.

In the end, Farmer Jack was happy because everything on the farm was quiet again.

The End

The Field Mouse Meets the House Mouse

One morning, Betty, the house mouse, was cleaning her mouse house. She heard a noise coming from the kitchen. It was her two brothers Bill and Will. They were all house mice. Bill and Will had been stealing cheese. Tom, the house cat, was chasing them around the kitchen. Betty came into the kitchen and asked, "What's going on in here?"

"We're only trying to get our breakfast. This overgrown flea bag will not let us," said her brother Bill.

"What's the matter, Tom?" asked Betty.

"They came in here making a lot of noise knocking over glasses and dishes," said Tom the cat.

"Let them eat their breakfast, and I'll make sure they clean up the mess," said Betty.

"Well, alright. But if they don't, out they go," said the big cat.

"Now eat your breakfast, and after you're done, clean up this mess," shouted Betty.

"Thanks sis. You're a doll," said Will.

Tom the cat likes Betty. She is a pretty mouse. She's the only one who can handle the big cat.

The next day, Will and Bill were in the backyard playing cowboy and Indian. Bill ran though the house, and Will ran behind him. "I'm going to scalp you," shouted Will. Bill ran behind Tom the cat that was in the living room fast asleep. Will came behind him, chasing Bill all around the room. Bill ran over the cat's head and woke up the big cat. Tom began to chase the two mice around the room.

"That's it for you two mice. I'm going to tear you into pieces," said the cat.

But the two mice were moving too fast, running through the living room and through the kitchen. They ran all around behind the house.

"I'll get you two mice," shouted the cat.

Will and Bill ran into the mouse hole. "Sis, save us. Save us from that big ugly cat!"

"What are you two doing now?" asked Betty

"Nothing," said Bill.

"We were only playing cowboy and Indian," said Will.

"In the house!" screamed Betty. "How many times have I told you two not to play cowboy and Indian in the house. I'm going out for a walk so you better stay in this hole until that cat takes off."

Betty went walking out in the garden. She was picking flowers and humming a song. A voice came out of the woods.

"You sing beautifully."

"Who are you?" asked Betty.

"I'm John, the field mouse. Who are you, may I ask?"

"I'm Betty, the house mouse."

"You're very pretty," said John. "May I join you?"

"Yes," said Betty.

"I sing also. May I sing you a song?" asked John.

"If you would like to," replied Betty smiling.

"You are the prettiest girl I've ever see. I want to take you in my arms and never let you go. Your hair is like gold. It shines like the stars at night. You are the prettiest girl I've ever seen. Let me see you tonight."

"That was beautiful," said Betty.

"I have to go now," said John. "I am working over in Mr. Crain's field. May I see you tonight? Where do you live?"

"I stay over there in that big house," said Betty. "But I have two brothers who live with me, and there is a big cat watching the house."

"Well, meet me out here," said John. "And go to the barn dance with me."

"Alright," said Betty.

"I will meet you here at 8 o'clock," said John.

At 8 o'clock Betty met John in the garden. They went to the barn dance. The place was packed, so John and Betty decided to leave early. They went back to the garden where they first met.

It was about 9 o'clock. "Did I tell you how beautiful you look tonight?" asked John.

"Yes you have two or three times," replied Betty. "It sure is pretty out here tonight. Let's go up to the house."

"Are you sure it's safe?" asked John.

"Yes. Everyone is asleep," said Betty.

So the two mice went to the house. They were expecting to spend a quiet evening alone. When they arrived at the house, everything was quiet. Then out of nowhere came Betty's two brothers, Bill and Will.

"Hi sis, who's that with you?" asked Bill.

"This is John," said Betty. "He works next door in Mr. Crain's field."

"So he is a field mouse," said Will.

"And he is also my date," replied Betty.

The next day John and Betty were out in the garden. Then Bill and Will came. "Hi sis," said the two mice. "I see you're with John the field mouse again," said Will.

"Yes I am," replied Betty.

"Are you in love with John, sis?" asked Bill.

"That isn't your business," said Betty.

"Yes, we are in love," said John, the field mouse.

Everything was quiet for about a minute.

"Bill, may I speak with you alone?" asked Will. "Do you know what this means?"

"Yes, I think I do," said Bill. "That big cat will get the best of us without Betty to protect us!"

"So what are we going to do about it?" asked Will.

"We will tell Tom that Betty is in trouble with Mr. Crain, and the field mouse is after her," replied Bill.

So the two mice left. They told Tom, the cat, about Betty and John.

That night John and Betty were outside sitting on the porch. Out of the front door came the big cat. He chased the field mouse around the house.

Stop! Betty shouted.

But the big cat did not listen. Off into the woods the mouse ran.

Betty was so angry she stormed into the house and into her rat hole.

"Bill, Will, get in here!"

Bill and Will were looking out of the front window.

"What did you tell that cat?" asked Betty angrily.

"Nothing," said Will.

"Stop lying," said Betty. "Now, talk Bill. I know you two."

"We told him that John was chasing you because you went into Mr. Crain's field," said Bill.

"How could you two do this to me?" asked Betty.

Both brothers sat with their heads down. "It was for your own good," said Will. "He is no good for you. He's just an old broken down field mouse."

"Who are you to tell me who am good for me?" Betty shouted.

So the next day, Betty was sitting on the front porch. She was waiting for John, but he did not show up. She thought that maybe the cat had eaten him. Then, Will and Bill came out onto the porch to join her.

"I'm really sorry about last night," said the two mice.

"I don't want to hear about you two being sorry." Betty ran into the house and into her room.

That night, John came to the house. He looked through the window and saw that the big cat was asleep. He went around to the kitchen window and saw Bill and Will playing. He went to the side of the house and knocked on Betty's wall.

"Who's there?" asked Betty.

"It's me, John."

"You came back. I thought you were dead!" cried Betty.

"I'm not," said John. "I lost the cat in the woods. I came to take you away. Will you go?" asked John.

"Yes I will," said Betty.

"I'll be back around 10 o'clock."

When everyone was asleep and Betty was ready, she and John ran away, eloped, and never returned.

Bill's Plan

The next day, Bill and Will were playing. They were running from one room to the other. They knocked a flower pot off of the dresser. It fell right next to Tom's head. Tom jumped up! "It's those two mice again." He chased the two mice around the room. Bill and Will ran into Betty's room.

"Betty! Betty! Help us!" the two mice cried.

But there was no one there.

"Where is she?" asked Will.

"I don't know," said Bill. "Look, here's a note!"

Bill and Will,

By the time you have read this letter, I will be far away from here.

John and I decided to elope so that we could be together.

Goodbye,
Love Betty.

"Elope!" Bill shouted. "She left with that field mouse. What are we going to do?"

"I'm not worried about her now," said Will. "What about the cat out there?"

"That's what I'm talking about," said Bill. "Without Betty, we are goners!"

"We have got to find her, Bill," said Will. "You stay here and try to get some food while that cat's asleep. I'll go look for Betty. I'll ask some of our friends if they have seen her."

Off Will went into the woods. He met Bo, a farm mouse.

"Hi Bo," said Will. "Have you seen my sister?"

"No," said Bo. "Isn't she at home?"

"No, she ran away with John the field mouse."

"I'll help you look for them," said Bo.

So off Will and Bo went, into the woods and over the field.

Back at the house Bill was waiting for Tom, the cat, to fall asleep. He waited and waited. The big cat finally went to sleep. Bill then ran into the kitchen. On the table was a chocolate cake. The mouse was eating the cake when he heard the cat coming.

"I've got you now mouse!" said the cat.

"No way," replied Bill. "You'll never catch me."

Bill ran into the mouse hole. The cat was coming behind Bill so fast, he could not slow up in time, and he hit the wall with a hard bang. The cat jumped up.

"I'll get you if it's the last thing I do!"

It was late in the evening, and Will had just arrived.

"Hi Will, any luck?" asked Bill.

"No luck," said Will, "we looked everywhere and could not find them."

"Well, I will look tomorrow while you stay here," said Bill.

The next morning Bill was out and on his way to look for his sister. Bill met Bo.

Hi, Bo!

"We looked everywhere yesterday and did not find them."

The two mice went off into the woods and over the field. They met Jerry the field mouse. Jerry told them that Bill's sister was living in Mr. Crain's barn.

"So that's where they went," replied Bill. "I have an idea. Come back to the house with me Bo, and I will explain it to you."

Meanwhile back at the house, Will was in the kitchen trying to find something to eat. The big cat heard him and chased him from room to room. Will then ran into his mouse hole. The cat was coming so fast he could not stop on time. He hit the wall with a hard bang again. I'll get those rats if it's the last thing I do," shouted the cat. Bill and Bo had arrived. "Did you find her?" asked Will. "No, but we know where she is staying," said Bo. "She's over at Mr. Crain's barn staying with the filed mouse," said Bill. "So that is where they went, Mr. Crain's barn," replied Will.

"What's your plan?" asked Bo.

"This is what we will do." Bill began to explain. "We'll leave the house and go stay with Bo. Then Betty will hear about it and come home."

"That's a good idea," Will reply.

"But how will Betty know you are not here?" asked Bo.

"We'll tell Jerry to tell her that the cat chased us away from home," said Bill.

So the two brothers left to go and stay with Bo.

Betty Comes Home

The next day Bill told Jerry about the plan. Jerry told John and Betty about the big cat running Bill and Will away from home.

"What are we going to do?" asked John.

"I'm going home," said Betty. "The cat won't mess with them while I'm there."

Back at the house, Mr. Smith came in the back door, and the big cat was lying on the floor asleep.

"You good-for-nothing cat, get up and get out of here! I don't need you anymore. There are no mice in here!" shouted Mr. Smith. So he kicked the big cat out of the door.

That evening after John and Betty arrived, John asked Betty, "Where is the cat? I don't see him around."

Mrs. Smith came into the living room. "Where is the cat?" she asked her husband.

"I kicked him out," said Mr. Smith.

"So that's where the cat is. Mr. Smith kicked him out," replied Betty.

"Since there are no mice, there is no use for a cat," said John.

"I'll go over and bring Bill and Will, back tomorrow," said Betty.

The next morning, Betty went to Bo's house to get Bill and Will.

"Hi sis!" shouted Bill. "Did you come for us?"

"Yes," replied Betty.

When they arrived at the house, John was waiting at the back door.

"Where is the cat?" Will asked.

"Mr. Smith kicked him out," John replied.

"It's not the same without the cat," said Bill.

"How can we get him back?" asked Will.

"When Mr. Smith sees us, he will go and get the cat. I have an idea how we can get Mr. Smith to get the cat back. We can invite a bunch of our friends over. When Mr. Smith sees them, he will have to get the cat."

The next day Bill told Bo about his plan. Bo told Jerry, and Jerry invited some of his friends over to the Smith's house. That evening the house was full of mice. There were house mice, field mice, and so on. They were in the kitchen and in the living room. Mrs. Smith went into the house, and mice were everywhere. She called her husband. Mr. Smith went running into the house.

"What is it my dear?" he asked.

"Look! There are mice everywhere! You better get the cat back!" shouted Mrs. Smith.

So Mr. Smith ran out of the house to look for the cat. Mr. Smith went into town. He saw the cat in a trash can with another cat. "I'll take both of them home with me. That will make my wife happy," said Mr. Smith. He gathered up the two cats and took them to his house. When he made it home, he let them go into the house. The cats chased the mice everywhere. Some of them ran out the door and back into the field. Some of the mice ran into the hole of Will and Bill.

Tom or Jinks

The next day everything was quiet. Mr. and Mrs. Smith were having breakfast. The two cats were in the living room asleep.

"What are we going to do with two cats?" asked Mrs. Smith. "One of them has to go."

"We will see which one of them is the best at chasing mice. The best cat stays," said Mr. Smith.

There were two mice in the kitchen. Jinks the big black cat came into the kitchen. He chased the two mice out of the back door and into the woods. Our cat Tom never did that before, said Mr. Smith. So we'll get rid of Tom. Mr. Smith went into the living room and took the big cat by the collar and kicked him out of the door. Bill and Will were looking out of their mouse hole. What are we going to do ask Will? That Mr. Jinks will get rid of all of us if he stays. I don't know what we are going to do reply Bill. The big black cat, Mr. Jinks was so tough. The mice could not come out of their holes. The next day, he ran off three more mice. What are we going to do about that cat?" asked Will.

"I don't know, but he sure is getting rid of our overnight guest," replied Bill.

"Well, that's one way to get rid of them. Now if we only could get rid of that cat. I know what we can do," said Bill.

"What?" asked Will?

"Let's send for our cousin Ben, the city mouse."

"Good idea, Bill," said Will. "Cousin Ben is strong and fast. He can run Mr. Jinks away and Tom can come back.

The City Mouse

The next week, Ben the city mouse, arrived.

"Hello, I'm Cousin Ben."

"Hi, I'm Will, and this is Bill. You two are having trouble with the cat?" asked Ben.

"Yes," replied Bill. "He's a tough cat. We want you to get rid of him so that Tom can come back home. Ben saw Mr. Jinks sleeping in front of the fire place. Ben went over to the big cat and pulled one of the whiskers off of his face. Mr. Jinks jumped up. Then Ben took him by the tail and swung him around and threw him though the window. The big cat did not know what had happened. So he jumped up and ran through the woods all the way back to town. Thanks Cousin Ben," shouted Bill and Will.

"You won't have any more trouble with that cat," said Ben.

"Where is Betty? I want to see her before I go back home."

"She lives in Mr. Crain's barn now," replied Bill. "Do you want me to show you the way?"

"No thanks. I'll find it myself," said Ben.

The Smiths were having dinner when Mr. Smith asked, "Where is the cat?"

"I don't know," replied Mrs. Smith.

"I'll bring him back tomorrow. So the next day Mr. Smith went into town. He looked everywhere for the big black cat but could not find him. Then he looked across the street and he saw Tom. Come on Tom, I'm taking you back home. Tom was glad to be home. He was in the living room resting when Bill and Will came walked over to him. Good to have your back home," said Will. We got your job back for you Tom. Aren't you glad?"

"Thank you Bill and Will," replied Tom. "And I'm going to keep my job. So backing into your hole you mice, I hate you to pieces. And stay there. What gotten into that cat asked Bill? He doesn't want to lose his job again replied Will. When Cousin Ben gets back, we'll get him to teach Tom a lesson," said Bill.

It was late when Ben returned to the house. The cat was chasing Bill and Will from room to room. Ben caught the cat by the tail and threw him against the wall; so the three mice ran to the mouse hole. The next day Tom the cat went into town to look for his friend Mr. Jinks. Hey! Jinks called Tom. Want to get even with that city mouse? "Yes!" replied Jinks. What's your plan? We both will go back to the house and when he comes out I'll chase him. If I can't handle him, you chase him. Together we can get rid of him.

After a short while the two cats returned to the house. The three mice were in the kitchen. Tom and Jinks chased the mice around the room. Will and Bill escaped to their hole. Ben was still running when he lost one of the cats in the big room. Ben took the cat by the tail and threw him up against the bed. Then Tom, the house cat entered the room. By this time, Mr. Jinks had gotten back up. Ben did not know what to do. The two cats had him cornered. Tom caught the mice by the tail and threw him out of the window. Ben then ran in the back door of his two cousin's house. What are we going to do now?" asked Bill.

"I don't know," replied Ben. "But I have to return home tomorrow. I'll try to come back in about two weeks."

The next morning Ben was on his way back home. Mr. Jinks was outside when Ben was leaving. He and Tom chased Ben through the woods. I hope Ben got away from those cats," said Will.

"Me too," replied Bill.

After a while the two cats returned. "Thanks for your help Jinks," said Tom.

"Any time you need me, I'll be around," said Jinks.

So off Jinks went on his way back to town.

The Birthday Party

A week later, Bill and Will were preparing for their birthday party. They are twins. Will was outside talking to Bo.

"Who are you inviting to the party?" asked Bo.

"We're going to invite Jerry because he helped us to find Betty. We are also inviting a lot of our other friends," Will replied. "You are invited too."

"Are Betty and John coming?" asked Bo.

"Yes," replied Will.

"Bo, Will! Come here," shouted Bill. "Let's go into the kitchen and get some cheese for the party.

So the three mice went into the kitchen to find some cheese for the party. Be quiet. Don't wake the cat," said Bill.

But Bo and Will did not listen. They were playing with the eggs on the table. Bo threw one to Will, and Will missed it. The egg hit the floor. The cat heard the noise and went running into the kitchen. Run for your life!" shouted Bill. "Here comes the cat!"

Bo took an egg and threw it into the cat's face. The big cat then jumped up on the table, but Bo had already jumped off and ran for the door. The cat threw an egg and knocked Bo down. The cat jump off the table, Will then hit him with a spoon. Will and Bill then ran through the door, grabbed Bo, and took him into their hole. The cat got his senses back and started chasing after the mice, but he was not fast enough. After a while, the cat calmed down and lay down on the floor.

"The cat is going back to sleep now," said Bill.

"Get out and let's get the cheese now," said Bo.

"We have to be careful," said Will.

When the three mice were on their way out, the big cat jumped up and chased them back into the mouse hole.

"What has gotten into that cat? He's never been that fast before," said Bill.

Then the cat nailed up the front of the mouse hole. What are we going to do now? We will have to go through the back door and go around to the kitchen. So they did. But the cat was waiting for them. He then chased them around the house. But the mice then ran into the hole. The cat then nailed the back door up also. What are we going to do ask Bo? We will find a way out said Will. It was almost time for the party to begin in the three mice's were still trapped inside. I have an idea said Bill. We'll take the bed, run it into the board until it breaks. So they did and finally the board broke. The mice were free again. They did the same thing to the back door too. After a while the entire guest had arrived. The big cat was outside. When he return to the house mice were every where. The cat ran out the door in into town, to find his friend. An hour later the two cats returned. They chased the mice everywhere, all around the room. Some of them ran home. Down the road they went as fast as they could. The party was over and Mr. Jinks had returned to town.

"That cat's not getting away with this, I'm going to show him who's the boss!" said Will. When the cat was asleep the two mice went into the kitchen. When Tom enters the kitchen Bill threw an egg and hit him in the face. The cat was so mad he began chasing the mice. The mice ran as fast as they could. But the big cat caught them. He kicked Will out the door. Then he kicked Bill out. "And stay out!" shouted the cat. The cat went around and nails the door of the mouse hold up. How are we going to get in? Bill asks. I don't know, said Will. I guess we'll have to stay with Betty.

Bill and Will Come Home

Bill and Will returned home. They went around to the back of the house and the door of their home was still nailed up. "What are we going to do?" asked Will. We will go down the chimney replied Bill. When the two mice reach the fireplace they saw the big cat asleep. The two mice then ran to their room. What are we going to do about that cat kicking us out asked Will? I have an idea said Bill. Bill and Will went over to where the cat was." Will!" Go to the barn to get a rope. When he returned they tied the rope to the cat tail. Bill jumped on the cat's back. Will pulled the cat whiskers the cat jump up and started chasing Will. Will ran half way across the room, with the cat chasing behind him. The rope stops the cat and he fell on his stomach. Bill jumped off the cat back and ran over to Will. The two mice went into the kitchen. Mrs. Smith had left a cake on the table. The two was eating cake while the cat was still struggling to get loose. After a while the cat got loose. He ran into the kitchen fast as he could. He jumps on the table and began to chase the mice. Will jump in a cup, Bill jump off the table and ran around the room, with the cat chasing behind him. Bill ran by the table, Will jump out of the cup and pushed the cake off the table and onto the cat. The cat was really mad now; he began throwing eggs at the mice.

The mice ran as fast as they could. One of the eggs hit Will in back of the head and knocked him into Bill. The cat then caught both mice by their tails. This time when I put you out, you'll not getting back in shouted the cat. Just as the cat open the door, Betty was standing in front of him. "Tom!" what are you doing? I'm about to get rid of your two brothers, replying the cat. Let them go, ill make sure they don't give you any more trouble. Betty and her two brothers went into their mouse hole. "Thank Sis!" said Bill. Are you home to stay asked Will? Yes, until spring said Betty. The next day everything was normal again. Bill and Will were playing cowboys and Indians and Betty was out in the flower garden. And the big cat was lying in front of the fire place asleep.

The End